T0104710

Roots in the Circles

Roots in the Circles

Voices of the Grandfathers

Gilles R. G. Monif, M.D

 iUniverse®

ROOTS IN THE CIRCLES
VOICES OF THE GRANDFATHERS

iUniverse books may be ordered through booksellers or by contacting:

iUniverse
1663 Liberty Drive
Bloomington, IN 47403
www.iuniverse.com
1-800-Authors (1-800-288-4677)

Because of the dynamic nature of the Internet, any web addresses or links contained in this book may have changed since publication and may no longer be valid. The views expressed in this work are solely those of the author and do not necessarily reflect the views of the publisher, and the publisher hereby disclaims any responsibility for them.

Any people depicted in stock imagery provided by Thinkstock are models, and such images are being used for illustrative purposes only. Certain stock imagery © Thinkstock.

ISBN: 978-1-4917-6753-5 (sc)
ISBN: 978-1-4917-6754-2 (e)

Library of Congress Control Number: 2015907344

Print information available on the last page.

iUniverse rev. date: 09/02/2015

Contents

Dedication

To the Sierra Club, The Nature Conservatory,
Defenders of the Environment, Green Peace,
John Muir, Robert Redford, Ted Turner and the
many whose respect for the Earth enriches us all.

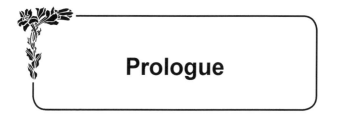

Prologue

On December 5, 1890: Chief Sitting Bull is killed by the Bureau of Indian Affairs (BIA) police. Fearing reprisals, 200 members of his Hunkpapa band flee the Standing Rock Reservation to join Chief Spotted Elk and his Miniconjou band at the Cheyenne River Reservation*.

On December 23, 1890: Joined by 38 Hunkpapa, Spotted Elk's group leaves the Cheyenne River Reservation to seek protection with Red Cloud at the Pine Ridge Indian reservation.

On December 28 1890, Chief Spotted Elk and approximately 350 of his followers composed of 120 men, and 230 women and children are intercepted by a Seventh Cavalry Detachment under Major Samuel M. Whiteside near Porcupine Bluff. The troopers escort the group to Wounded Knee where they are told to make camp. Later that evening, the rest of the Seventh Calvary, commanded by Colonel James W. Forsyth, arrive. Spotted Elk's camp is surrounded. Four rapid fire Hotchkiss guns are set up on high ground overlooking the Indian encampment*.

Gilles R. G. Monif, M.D

On December 29, 1890: Colonel Forsyth orders surrender of all weapons in preparation of removal and transportation of the Indians from the area of military operation. D Troops of the Seventh Calvary enter the encampment and begin the search for weapons. A scuffle occurs between an old warrior who has a rifle in his hand and two soldiers. Armed conflict quickly ensues. The Hotchkiss guns decimate the campsite in less than ten minutes. A large number of women and children try to escape by running and scattering in a ravine or over the prairie. Of the original 350 Native Americans, 4 men and 47 women and children initially survive. Seven of these 51 survivors subsequently die*.

The Seventh Calvary lost 25 men. Another 39 were wounded (6 fatally). Most of the soldiers in company D were killed by friendly fire from the four Hotchkiss guns*.

Edward S. Godfrey; Commander, D Company, Seventh Calvary*

"I don't believe they saw their sights. They fired rapidly but it seemed to me only a few seconds until there was not a living thing before us: warriors, squaws, children, ponies, and dogs... went down before the unaimed fire."

Hugh McGinnis; First Battalion K Company, Seventh Calvary*

"Following a three day blizzard, General Nelson A Miles visited the scene of carnage. He estimated that around 300 snow shrouded forms were strewn over the countryside. He discovered to his horror, among the dead lay the bodies of children and women with babies in their arms who had been chased as far as two miles from the original scene of encounter and cut down without mercy by the troops."

American Horse, Oglala Lakota*

"There was a woman with an infant in her arms who was killed as she almost touched the flag of truce. ... A mother was shot down with her infant; the child not knowing that its mother was dead was still nursing... The women, as they were fleeing with their babies, were killed .... And after most of all of them had been killed, a cry was made that all those who were not killed or wounded should come forth and they would be safe. Little boys .... came out of their place of refuge, and as soon as they came in sight, a number of soldiers surrounded them and butchered them there."

General Miles denounced Colonel Forsyth and relieved him of his command. Subsequently, Forsyth was promoted to Major General. Twenty Medals of Honor were awarded to members of the Seventh Calvary.

CIRCLES

September 11, 1975, Pine Ridge Reservation

Surrounded on one side by a curving ravine filled with cedar and scattered cottonwood trees, the house has stood, seemingly forever, on top of the hill. A north wind finds its voice as it moves the branches of the trees.

Originally built for General Cooke's designee, its hard white pine construct has outlasted the many years of Dakota winters. With two coats of paint and a new roof, doors and windows, it again houses an individual of prominence, Georges Mehel, former World Court Justice.

The reception area has been transformed into an impressive library. Walnut floor-to-ceiling built-in bookshelves cover the greater part of three walls. Within the remaining spaces hang a series of photographs portraying eleven or more men in long black robes and photographs of him with world dignitaries. The reception area flows into what had been the dining room. A large mahogany desk dominates the room.

In front of the desk are two wooden high-back chairs. Stacks of folders and papers crowd the green leather insert of the desk.

The former World Jurist is seated with his back to the desk, immersed in the documents in his hand. His long salt-and-pepper hair come down and meets at its end.

Well into her fifties, Martha Songbird quietly enters the room carrying a tray. The tray contains what is a nearly nightly ritual: a small bowl of fresh mulberries and pecans, several pieces of fried bread, a cup containing honey and a spoon along with an earthen teapot, cup and saucer.

Martha Songbird asks "Where do you want me to put your evening tea?"

World Jurist Mehel is slow in finishing with the document in his hand. Still holding the case file, he turns around. Looking up he realizes that Martha has been standing there longer than a few seconds. "Sorry. The usual place," motioning to a small matching mahogany table to his right.

Martha slowly makes her way around the corner of the desk. She sets the tray on the table that already is burdened with the day's mail. Noting that he has yet to open any of the letters in the afternoon mail, she takes it upon herself to screen them. Her hand stops on a linen envelope whose return address she already knows.

"There is a letter from your son."

Georges quickly gets up from the large leather chair and walks towards Martha's extended hand.

He towers a good foot over Martha Songbird. His body build is that of a decade or more younger man.

Opening the letter with his finger, he first reads its contents to himself. Turning to Martha he recites fragments for her benefit: "As a child, White Cloud taught me the Legend of the Dream Catcher. Iktomi says that if you believe in the Great Mystery, the web will catch your good ideas and let the bad ones pass harmlessly through the hole at its center. The evil within Native American dreams cannot escape through the center of the web. It's closed!"

He returns to reading the letter to himself before again addressing Martha.

"Don't delude yourself into thinking that all your Harvard and Oxford degrees constitute a bullet-proof vest. Mediocrity understands but one thing: if you can't compete with a standard, destroy it."

Shaking his head, Georges puts the letter down and turns back towards the desk.

"Martha, his soul is still not moving in a good direction."

Martha waits a long moment before asking, her tone sympathetic, "If there is nothing more you need, I'll be going."

"Good night Martha." Then breaking free of his thoughts, Georges inquires "Do you want me to drive you?"

Martha interrupts. "I have the car tonight Mr. Mehel. I'll be fine." She pats the sheathed knife under her shirt, strapped to her right thigh.

Carefully, Martha locks both double-bolt locks of the front door.

Carrying a bundle of food, she descends the newly rebuilt porch steps and slowly walks to a car that is making the transition from steel to rust. Like her the old Ford had forgotten about dying gracefully.

She opens the door of the car. A small dream catcher hangs from the mirror. Martha gets in and starts reaching for the door handle to close it. Realizing that night crickets had suddenly stopped signing, Martha freezes for a moment. Instinctively her free hand quickly unsheathes her knife.

Hand brake off, the car silently rolls down the hill and slides unto a gravel road before Martha tries to start the car. On a second try, the engine responds. Instead of heading south as she always does to go home, the car turns north.

Parked on the hill's crest, the car's headlights flash seven times in the direction of the darkness below.

Former World Court Justice, Georges Snow Eagle Mehel never heard the second bolt turn and the door open.

Moments later, his blood, slowly spreading on the desk, contrasts with its green leather insert.

September 12, 1975, New York City

The midtown New York skyline is on display as the evening cleaning crews work to prepare the buildings for another day of occupancy.

A tall dark-skinned man with jet black hair dressed in a white silk shirt and dark trousers turns away from the large bay window on the fortieth floor. Putting down the New York Times on the reading table next to his personal comfort chair, he slowly walks to the telephone and picks it up.

The voice on the other end asks, "May I please speak to Mr. Isaiah Mehel. This is Captain Owen Fritz of the South Dakota State Patrol calling."

The next words are "I'm sorry to inform you that your father is dead".

Isaiah continues to listen. His face tightens. His eyes close.

The next statement from the South Dakota sends the phone crashing into the receiver.

Responding to the noise, Christina moves to the bathroom door. The light penetrates her sheer dressing gown, silhouetting her long slender body. "What's wrong?" When there is no immediate response to her question, she repeats the question, but now with urgency. "Isaiah, what's wrong?"

"They shot him."

Christina comes quickly and presses her body against him. She starts to speak. His hand cups over her mouth as if to say not now. The whiteness of her skin makes his hand look even darker. Her long blonde hair pressed against his chest contrasts with the blackness of his.

After a long moment, Christina disengages. "Who are they?"

Isaiah, not ready to answer, takes a deep breath. He turns away from Christina and crosses over to the wooden magazine rack next to the over-sized arm chair he had previously occupied. He reaches down, removes a copy of the New York Times, opens it to a back page, folds it lengthwise, and presents it to Christina.

The bold print of the article reads "Pine Ridge Reservation: Murder Capital of the United States."

Isaiah's voice is not one of hurt, but more of a subdued anger. "Nothing has changed since Wounded Knee."

Sensing her confusion, he bends and kisses her forehead before again settling into his big overstuffed chair.

"This is just one more circle within other circles whose completion is usually paid in blood.

My grandmother's father was a Miniconjou who had joined Spotted Elk's group at ….. But that was a long time ago."

Abruptly, Isaiah drops the subject.

"My grandfather was said to have been someone of standing in the Lakota Nation: a man of standing who won one too many fights; or so the story is told. A tribal member, probably drunk, got into a fight with three men in one of the towns bordering the reservation. He intervened too successfully. A shotgun was retrieved by one of the beaten men from his truck and then used to kill.

A year later, my grandmother's tuberculosis became terminal. Jamel Mehel, a physician working for the Indian Health Service and his wife, Martha, took my father off the reservation, but never from the reservation. Until he was fourteen, his summers were spent on the reservation. Private schooling and athletics paved his way to Harvard. Minority status, intelligence and athletics, ultimately made him a unique addition to Harvard Law School."

My story began between Harvard and Harvard. My mother was the rebellious daughter of a wealthy business man. Wealthy was and is an understatement. What shouldn't have happened happened: a nine pound, four ounce, six month old "premature" who is much too dark. Her family never accepted the marriage. … or me."

Isaiah is interrupted by an aggressive misuse of the door buzzer.

Isaiah and Christina look at each other for a moment before Isaiah emphatically states. "Mother!"

Christina quickly goes to the hall closet and pulls out a black rain coat. Putting it on over her nightgown, she reaches for the door locks.

The ringing of the door buzzer is now replaced by two sharp raps on the door.

The apartment door is opened.

There stands Rebecca in a mink coat with sable collar and trim. In her late fifties, she stands there, emblematic of wealth's attempt to defy age.

The two women look at each other for a long moment; then Rebecca marches past Christina into the room.

She looks at Isaiah. "You've heard, haven't you?" Sensing that no answer is immediately forthcoming, Rebecca continues. "Damn it. I told them not to call you until they heard from me! I wanted to be here when you got the news."

Rebecca loosens her mink coat as she moves further into the living room and faces Isaiah. "Before you say anything, I want you to know that there was a time when I truly did love your father. This demand from White Cloud that you go to that ugly place to bury him is just out of the question. If your father hadn't insisted on it in the divorce agreement, you would have never been forced to go there."

Isaiah is quick to respond. "What demand from White Cloud?"

Confused, Christina interrupts. "Rebecca, what are you two talking about?"

"You don't know, do you?"

Rebecca takes off her full length coat and throws it unto an adjacent small table. Seeing Isaiah's arm chair to be empty, she promptly seats herself in it. "I don't know how much Isaiah has or has not told you about his youth."

"About his early childhood, not much. The rest I know".

"Well, it goes like this. Georges was at Harvard Law School and I was at Radcliff. Isaiah's father was a very handsome man. Everything might have been different where it not for World War II. Georges had made a place for himself within one of New York's largest legal firms that was tied to Rothschilds. The rumors of the persecution and atrocities were already being whispered. For him, what was happening in Europe was the worst type of crime against his damn Hoop of Nations".

Looking at Isaiah, "Anyway, you probably need to know this. The night before he left, he woke me up.

"In my son, you have given me the greatest gift a man can receive. By having planted my seed into the earth, I'm free in front of the shadow of death and ..."

"I didn't want to hear what I already knew was in his heart. For him, the embers of Wounded Knee had now a twentieth century location. By his choice and not mine, he disappeared into the clandestine world of O.S.S.

I could not hold him and I really tried."

Rebecca's voice betrays her growing emotional discomfort. Sensing that, Christina asks if she would like coffee.

Rebecca starts to say no, but then reconsiders. "That would be fine."

Focusing on Isaiah, Rebecca continues. "His letters were so heavily censored as to be nearly unreadable."

Rebecca reaches for her large black leather pursue and withdraws what looks like paper fragments that have been pasted to an 8 x 11 sheet of paper. She begins reading as much to herself as to Isaiah: "Behind the German lines, I'm more than a spectator to death .... I have to fight not to rejoice when the enemy faileth by my hand .... To surmount my fear of death I have surrendered my soul to belief in the Great Mystery."

Rebecca pauses. Then with a deep sigh, she says "I was sure he was going to die....."

Christina returns with a tray bearing three cups of coffee. Rebecca takes her cup. Needing an ally, she indicates for Christina to take the seat closest to her.

"When for almost a year, I heard nothing. Just nothing! My father used his connections to have Georges declared legally dead. Isaiah was three when we moved to the big house and…."

Isaiah, who has remained standing all this time, interrupts "And at four, I had a brother."

Rebecca shoots Isaiah a look of displeasure. "Satire comes from the Greek word for tearing of flesh. Well the same goes for what you just said. That was hurtful."

Rebecca turns back to Christina. "Georges' reappearance caused more than an inconvenience. Things had gone too far in another direction. The only thing he asked was that, every year until the age of twelve, Isaiah be sent back to the reservation and tutored by White Cloud, the son of his spiritual teacher.

After the war, his transfer from O.S.S. to JAG is how he became involved with the Nuremberg Trials and ultimately with the World Court at The Hague."

Rebecca turns to Isaiah who by now is back standing by the bay window overlooking a darkened New York skyline. "I'm not going, so don't ask me to."

Isaiah turns to face Rebecca. "You don't have to and neither do I. According to the South Dakota Police, last night his body has disappeared from the morgue in Rapid City.

What is this about White Cloud demanding?"

Rebecca, realizing that she had revealed something that she did not intend to, chooses not to respond.

Looking at Isaiah with concern, Christina asks "Are you going to go?"

Isaiah's mood grows darker. "I don't know; more important, why."

Christina answers for him. "Because he is your father!"

With muted anger, Isaiah responds. "He was my father, but he always belonged to them and their obsession with justice and respect. Wounded Knee was so embedded in his psyche that there was little to no room for me. They should have never taken him from the reservation and exposed him to the world beyond.

He was never really there when I needed him."

November 14, 1969, Wallingford, Connecticut

Madeleine Closter walks into the Headmaster's office. "The gentleman from the World Court is here."

"Please show him in."

As Madeleine ushers the visitor in, he gets up from his chair and walks forward, hand outstretched.

"After several years of correspondence, it is a pleasure to meet you in person. I'm only sorry the circumstances could not be different. Please be seated, indicating a large leather chair.

As you have been informed, there was a fight. Two of the three other individuals involved are requiring rather extensive medical care. One of those involved was also a student at this school. Since your son plays football, this puts the school in an awkward position."

Georges Mehel lets an almost imperceptible smile flicker for a moment before sitting down. "I appreciate the school's position. I can only apologize for my son's behavior."

He pauses. "I understand that a verbal exchange preceded the incident."

The sensitivity of the subject about to be discussed causes the Headmaster a moment of anguish. "Your information is correct, but ….."

Georges Mehel interrupts, all while removing official looking papers from his briefcase. "My son is a young man who is perhaps overly sensitized to his mixed cultural background.

Individuals acting on my behalf have obtained five depositions from witnesses. They corroborate the initiation of the conversation by the three other individuals, the use of racial and ethnic slurs, and the throwing of a bottle containing alcohol. My son is guilty, but guilt must be proportionally shared."

Without looking at the documents in his hand, the Headmaster replies, "Your former wife's father, his other grandfather has….."

Again Georges interrupts "Before money transforms the incident into a non-event and destroys its lesson, let me suggest the following: football out and temporary suspension for both students lest someone misinterpret the message."

Surprised at the bluntness of the proposal, the school's Headmaster smiles. "So it will be."

Georges Mehel gets up. "I apologize for my brevity, but I must return to the World Court in less than 23 hours. May I see him?"

"Please use my office." The Headmaster walks to the door which, when opened reveals Isaiah standing there.

Isaiah storms into the room. The door closes behind him with more than normal emphasis. "I don't need one of your shit-ass lectures. Nobody gets to pick where he is born and the baggage that comes with it."

Pausing for but a second, "Our conversations, if a one sided dialogue can ever be called a conversation, are always lectures about what I should do, who I should be, and my Lakota heritage. Your damn Lakota dreams are a pathway to destruction. Literally, you have been asking me to cross a rope bridge that spans a bottomless canyon. Its ropes are badly frayed. When the bridge loses its ties to your Mother Earth, its pendulum will swing down into nothingness."

Calmly, Georges begins. "I understand your anger. I have been touched by similar fires, but when you give in to anger, you have lost. Don't use the conflicts of your birth to justify your actions in this matter. I am truly sorry that you have had to face the harsh north wind alone; but that does not justify your using the power of the Bear instead of the wisdom of the Owl."

Georges voice becomes more severe and his facial expression more resolute. "Ethnocentric racism is a disease to which you must build immunity but NEVER tolerance!"

Isaiah explodes. "You're a fucking black hole! You have always been a large figure in the mist. Your persona cuts like a knife, leaving no ragged edges. I can hear you. I can touch you, but there are times I don't know if you are real."

The alarm of Georges' pocket watch sounds. The delays at the airport have cost him precious time.

"At the time the arrangements for your education were made, they were in your best interests. In the underpinnings of the war, I saw elements that, if not challenged, could ultimately destroy the Hoop of Nations.

If the ropes of the bridge that you speak of do break, destruction will ultimately consume, not just the Lakota, but all within the Hoop of Nations. My life journey has been a battle that I could not take you on then for multiple reasons.

Time forces me to terminate this so-called "shit-ass" conversation. Your stupidity will probably cost you admission to medical school. In the future, when tempted to use the strength of the Bear, do as I have done and channel your anger into a creative force in the service of a Higher Power."

September 14, 1975, New York City

As Isaiah walks by his secretary, she intercepts him. "Good morning, Mr. Mehel," "I am truly sorry to hear about your dad. That was a wonderful article about him in yesterday's New York Times.

I bought five copies for your files."

"Thank you Gilha."

As Isaiah is about to enter his office, she adds, "UPS just delivered a package for you."

Jokingly, she adds, "It looks like it could bite".

"Thank you for the heads up and again for the papers."

Sitting on his large, highly polished cherry wood desk is a box that looks like something salvaged from a dumpster. The postmark reads South Sioux City, Nebraska. The box is held together by a string composed of white, yellow, red and black strands. Finding the letter opener inadequate for the task, Isaiah reaches into a bottom drawer, retrieving a small knife whose handle is made from part of a deer's antler.

The box's contents are composed of newspaper clippings about the American Indian Movement (AIM), the recent uprising on the Pine Ridge Reservation and the killing of two FBI agents. Isaiah quickly scans the box's contents. As he empties the box's contents into a wastepaper basket, a tan unopened envelope with a painted falcon feather catches his attention. He reaches down and retrieves the discarded.

Isaiah cuts open the envelope. He reads:

"The Elders have determined that you are the one to deliver your father to the Great Mystery.

You are to buy tickets from New York City to Cleveland and from Cleveland to Sioux Falls, South Dakota in someone else's name. Then, buy another set of tickets in your name whose final destination is Cedar Rapids, South Dakota.

Be careful. The reservation is a killing field. Two FBI agents have been killed in a gun battle. The revenge that couldn't be done legally is being done by Dick Wilson's paramilitary force, Guardians of the Ogallala Nation (GOONs). More than 60 opponents of the BIA (Bureau of Indian Affairs) have died violent deaths. Killings are being met with killings. Returning to Pine Ridge may be the most dangerous of your Four Hills that you are traveling."

Isaiah is about to discard the opened envelope when a small photograph of a young man and a very young boy falls out of it. He picks up the photograph and studies it for a long moment, He then reaches down and retrieves the clippings from the trash. As he re-reads them, Isaiah thinks to himself 'Why would anyone care about a ritual for a man whose physical body no longer exists?'

Isaiah finishes reading the newspaper clippings. Taking a large envelope from a file cabinet, he carefully puts them in. He is about to close the file cabinet drawer, when Sol Horowitz, a man in his mid-fifties, almost bald, opens the door and walks in.

"Sorry about your other dad. A judge at the World Court in The Hague. Quite an achievement for an Indian! You should have brought him around."

Sol walks over to Isaiah's desk and takes a thin cigar out of the wooden humidor and lights it.

"Tell me which church and I'll have Ruthie send flowers from the Firm."

Isaiah shakes his head. "First, Sol there is no physical church to speak of and, second, the humidor is not a candy box."

"You know, but I can't resist a good Cuban cigar. I presume that you'll need a few days off. But remember, you're lead counsel before the New York Appellate Court in the Monsanto case. That's in less than ten days. This is time to be ranking up billable hours. OK?"

Not exactly pleased, Isaiah doesn't answer. He walks away from Sol and looks out the window for a long minute.

"Sol, ever been to an Indian Reservation?"

Laughing, Sol replies. "Are you kidding? Never have and never will".

"You haven't missed much. Reservation towns are pretty much the same: old men sitting, waiting for little more than a tomorrow that will never come: a nation killing time and itself with cheap liquor.

Even when nature's beauty returns to the place, what you have are prefabricated houses, dilapidated trailers and rusting shells of cars waiting for yet another winter's snow to come. It's little more than an attempt at spiritual living amidst its physical dying."

Finally Isaiah turns. "OK....., but not OK.

As for billable hours, don't worry, the firm's client will be appropriately raped. But I'm going to need seven days! Before you get something stuck in the wrong orifice, tomorrow, you'll have two letters on your desk: one to the Clerk of the Appellate Court requesting a rescheduling of the hearing; the other my resignation from the firm. It's for you to determine which letter rules."

"Oh, bullshit. You're the youngest partner in this firm. Cut the dramatics. You're not going to chuck six figures out the window."

"Right but. One he is my father. More importantly, someone has called in an old debt that I have little choice but to honor."

21

May 7, 1936, Pine Ridge Reservation

Twelve year old Isaiah walks ten steps behind a taller, athletic White Cloud. Both figures are making their way up a sinuous mountain path somewhere in the Black Hills of South Dakota.

Isaiah's body language is a mixture of boredom and anger. Reaching down, he snaps a young sapling growing along the trails edge from its roots.

Observing what has just happened White Cloud asks "What do you have in your hands?"

Surprised that his action had been noticed, Isaiah looks at the object in his hand for a long second before answering. "A plant. No a tree."

"What is wrong with your tree?"

Still surprised, Isaiah takes a long pause in which he searches for the right answer. "It has no roots."

"What happens to trees without roots?"

Isaiah looks down and does not answer.

White Cloud continues. "Trees are special to us. We call them standing people. We are like trees. We have trunks; branches like arms, hair like leaves, but lack roots necessary to anchor us in Mother Earth so as to be able to spiritually touch Father Sky."

Looking Isaiah directly in the eyes. "Where are your roots?"

When there is no response from Isaiah, White Cloud continues. "Life consists of two worlds: the life within and the outward body. Physical existence has little meaning. Your life is the opportunity to connect the two, but to do so you must find your true roots."

September 17, 1975, Sioux Falls, South Dakota

The Sioux Falls airport is small, making locating the men's room easy. As instructed, Isaiah enters. Once inside, a well-dressed, dark-skinned man in a three piece suit with a hand signal indicates that he is to enter the middle stall.

No sooner does he enter, but a worn cloth bag slides under an adjacent partition. Isaiah extracts money, notepad, keys, and tobacco from his black leather overnight bag. His tailor-made Harris tweed jacket, trousers, silk shirt, Van Pell shoes and tie are exchanged for lined jeans, a heavy red flannel shirt, a cloth bag, worn boots, and a hat complete with instructions that it be worn at all times while in the airport.

Having completed White Cloud's instructions to the letter, Isaiah exits the stall and proceeds to wash his hands. He is totally amused at White Cloud's detailed instructions. "White Cloud's paranoia is making something simple unnecessarily complicated. Does he really think that a government cares about any funeral but its own?"

Just then, two men in suits enter the facility. In the mirror, Isaiah watches when one of the men points out to the other his highly polished shoes and dropped pants which are discernible behind the door next to the one Isaiah has just vacated.

Exiting the Men's Room, Isaiah takes a moment to get his bearings. Then, he identifies the north exit. Once outside, things move quickly. A faded, dark blue sedan emerges out of seemingly nowhere. Still rolling, the back door is thrust open. The words, "Get in", say all that is needed.

Within a few minutes, it is apparent that no one is going to be able to follow this car. At every second or third block a sharp turn is made. One set of eyes is always focused on the back window. Once in the industrial part of Sioux Falls, a high speed left turn is made. The car comes to an abrupt stop. Isaiah and his back seat companion jump out, run down a narrow alley, and stop at the side door of the warehouse.

When the door is opened, Isaiah stands facing a man that he had not seen for twenty years. Running Deer embraces Isaiah. Federal surplus food had added some pounds to his short, but muscular build. Isaiah is slow to respond. The long scar above his left cheekbone had not faded with time. On the reservation, Running Deer had been his major protagonist in the game "throw from horses". Within a minute, two more faces from his past appear.

His grey hair at shoulder length, White Cloud takes his time walking stiffly around a large white delivery van. The leg wound had not healed. Isaiah is taken back. White Cloud has so aged. His skin tells of time spent outdoors. Creases of age and worry now occupy spaces previously smooth. As if parting had never been, the two embrace. Opening the van's rear door, White Cloud says "Get in. We have a long drive. There is much to talk about."

The back of the van has been restructured. Two long benches line the windowless walls. The cartons containing water, fried bread, and deer or buffalo jerky do little to detract from guns stacked in the middle of the floor. Four more Native Americans join the group. What surprises Isaiah is that only one of the now six occupants is a Lakota Sioux.

The reservation had not carried into his other world. But as he sits there next to White Cloud, the full impact of that telephone call hits him. Physically he is about to be transported to a past, long buried. At some point in his obligated duty, he'll be asked to mentally cross back into that which he had long abandoned."

Once the van's doors close, Isaiah takes from his cloth bag cut tobacco and cigarettes which are passed around to the van's occupants.

For a while no one speaks.

White Cloud breaks the silence. "Do you know why he came back?"

White Cloud's question arouses Isaiah from self-absorbing thoughts.

White Cloud does not wait for an answer. "For him, the difference between the massacre at Wounded Knee and the Holocaust are but one of scale. Both are examples of a false pride that denies the humanity of man within the Hoop of Nations. He knew coming back to be a warrior, but now with a pen, would eventually cost him his life. I don't think he imagined that it would be so soon. Did you carefully read all the articles I sent you?"

Isaiah does not answer. White Cloud seemingly understands the significance of his silence.

"The second coming of Wounded Knee had had the potential of another massacre. Rifles and shotguns have never been a match for armored personnel carriers and armed helicopters. All who gathered at Pine Ridge Reservation were resolute in purpose, knowing it could mean death. Only fear of world condemnation kept a massacre from re-occurring at Wounded Knee.

Once the so-called Pine Ridge uprising was crushed, just as it was for those of the Ghost Dances some eighty years previously, the government set out to destroy its leaders. A movement without leaders is not a threat. Your father came to war against the racial bigotry that covers us like the black dust of the Plains. He was determined to prevent the voices of protest from being crushed into silence and to preserve the few freedoms we have been granted. As judged by history, we are the longest prisoners of war in the world. Our lands have been taken. The treaties of peace are but documents of betrayal. Our way of life and our spirituality trivialized."

White Cloud stops.

The confined rear portion of the van has gone past being warm. Without ventilation, the van is becoming uncomfortable. Isaiah's flannel shirt has long since joined the cartons on the floor.

White Cloud closes his eyes and rests. The hours creep forward. Periodically, someone reaches for the fried bread or jerky. The space within the van no longer tolerates smoking.

Isaiah takes the opportunity to close his eyes and is soon asleep.

White Cloud's voice and a not so small nudge bring Isaiah back to the present.

"When the American Indian Movement developed, it bred a new consciousness into our lives. Everything AIM does or will do is to reclaim our dignity as members within the Hoop of Nations.

Let me paint for you an example or in your strange language, a case-in-point. In symbolic protest of the 1868 treaty that had been imposed by force of arms, AIM decided that during the upcoming trials of its leaders, no Native American would stand when a judge entered a courtroom.

Some weeks ago when Native Americans failed to respond to the bailiff's "*please rise*', a state judge in Sioux Falls decided that he would not tolerate this insubordination. He warned the defense counsels, that they, their clients, and their supporters would be held in contempt if they did not rise when he entered the courtroom. The next day, when only an isolated individual responded to "*please rise*", the judge ordered the deputies and state police to "*make them rise*". A bloody fight erupted.

It may be many months before they hold another trial in that house of injustice."

Sensing that he is still listening, White Cloud continues.

"In the federal trial of another AIM member, upon learning of AIM's decision and its reason, the federal judge instructed his bailiff not to use "*please rise*".

Given what had recently happened, the tension surrounding that trial had built to a toxic level. To quote a newspaper account '*The courtroom was packed with AIM members. They had rabbit fur in their braids and porcupine quills in their vests*'.

Most of the spectators and reporters left the courtroom quickly. Those who did not have that luxury bore white knuckles. The federal marshals present had radioed for backup. Even as Judge Odum entered the courtroom, the sounds of the state police running up the stairs could be heard.

A reporter who had stayed caught the moment. '*Once the judge came through the door and was seated, a courtroom packed with the militancy of AIM, fresh from battle, rose as if they were one and stood for a federal judge who had shown them integrity and honor.*'

For us, courts are not where justice is dispensed; merely a place where there is a remote chance of justice, especially when you are legally a prisoner of war."

Again time and close quarters extract their toll.

Isaiah's white Brooks Brothers undershirt is now a shared towel of a slightly different color. Bottles of water are as likely to be poured on one's head as drunk. The trip is stripping everyone down to common essentials.

Having finished for the moment, it becomes White Cloud's time to eat, and above all drink. Isaiah's attention strays from one occupant to another. Seated in a back corner is the Lakota who is older than everyone else except possibly White Cloud. With his shirt off, Isaiah sees something that he recognizes. The blue ribbon around his neck is worn and faded. Its condition does little to diminish the significance of what rests on his bare chest nor the barrel of a World War II carbine in his right hand.

White Cloud takes his time getting to the final subject. He puts down an empty bottle of water and finishes the last bit of buffalo jerky.

"We are a conquered people who have had the imprint of our heroes taken from us. That of your father's shall not be one more. The government is determined that his legacy does not become as inspiration source for any of us." Unconsciously, White Cloud's right hand tightens on the gun in his lap.

"Our oral history speaks of a Power Place where the remains of Crazy Horse, Red Cloud, and others lie safe from the desecration of their remains and of their deeds as men and warriors. The Elders have decreed that you are the one who must release his soul from his body to the Great Mystery."

For Isaiah, the body having disappeared from the coroner's office is no longer a mystery. Somewhere deep in the Dakota Badlands, he envisions his father's physical body waiting high on a wood scaffold.

His tutorial begins again. "When you have been prepared, you will enter the Scared Circle of Life. Its four portals are its horizontal plane; the earth and the sky are its vertical plane. Together they are the base of the cosmic design of the universe. It is you who must ground for him ordinary space into its cosmos of timelessness.

To do so, you enter through the eastern portal. Someone will be there to point the way. You will...."

Three sharp raps on the panel separating Running Deer from its occupants. Guns and their intended users become one. Tense minutes slowly pass. Finally three series of double raps. Most, but not all, of the guns return to their previous resting places. The danger has apparently passed.

White Cloud lets time have its calming effect on everyone before continuing. Again addressing Isaiah, "You will enter from the East. The circle requires that you journey to the South Portal where you must speak of its power in terms of your father's life. Once done, you proceed to the Circle's West Portal and repeat the process. Then, the North Portal. When you return to the portal through which you entered, empty your heart. Then, you can leave: you having been cleansed of bad dreams and your father's spirit being free to fly among the eagles."

The hum of underinflated tires is now gone, having been replaced by bumps and jolts. No one's seat is permanent. Branches strike against the truck's side. Suddenly, the van stops. Multiple voices are heard outside.

The rear door suddenly swings open. A gun which had been on the floor is in Isaiah's right hand. The safety is off.

 **ROOTS**

September 18, 1975, Black Hills

White Cloud's hand lowers the barrel of Isaiah's gun. "We have arrived. This is where you and I must part. Physically, I can't make the next part of the journey with you. You'll be with our cousins, the Oglala. Broken Lance will be your companion from here on out. Go quickly to the trees. The horses are waiting".

The truck backs up. Quickly, White Cloud gets back in. Running Deer waves. Then, they are gone. As the dust settles, Isaiah acutely feels his isolation.

Binoculars hanging from his neck, from afar Broken Lance motions for Isaiah to come quickly into the cover. "So far no helicopters, he says, "but we still need to wait until dusk."

Broken Lance is a few years younger and a head shorter than Isaiah.

He points to a smallish grey Arabian. "He's yours. In the bag behind the saddle, you'll find extra clothes, thermoses and food. I'd take a good long piss before you put these on." He hands Isaiah long johns and a padded jacket.

"When the sun disappears, you will know the cold."

For Isaiah, the thought of colder air is welcomed.

September 15, 1975, Arlington, Virginia

In Arlington, Virginia, National Security Director, Tom Bass, again looks through the personnel folder before placing it back in the front drawer of his ornate mahogany desk.

At thirty-five years old, Maureen MacLand is both the first female and possibly the youngest person to have achieved such a prominent position within the agency. She had been a legacy: the daughter of the Head of the House's Appropriation Committee and the granddaughter of the founder of The Greater America Foundation.

Her rapid ascension through the "company" had had several accelerants. Her psychological profile characterized her as being highly intelligent, self-motivated, decisive in her actions, and ambitious, but having difficulty with authority figures. A claim of gender bias had been lodged by her against the head of her first unit. The company having long been good-old boys club, her allegations were nominally investigated and accepted. The individual named was relieved of his duties. The subsequent allegation of sexual harassment was more troublesome. The charge could have been career ending had not the company's confidential files indicated that the individual's sexual preference was not that of women.

In both instances, her removal from the respective units came via promotions. Her allegations had carried the potential of consequences imposable by a *deus ex machina* in Congress and a grandfather who controls one of Washington's more powerful think tanks.

September 18, 1975, Arlington, Virginia

Normally worn in a bun, her long blond hair loosely flows around her shoulders. Her skirt is noticeably an inch or two shorter than usual. As Operations Director for the Midwest, Maureen knows she is in trouble, deep trouble.

Just before entering the Director's Office, she double checks her attire.

The response to her cheerful "Good morning Tom" is anything but warm.

"Sit down!"

"What happened to please? Did it go on vacation or something?", she asks in a joking tone of voice.

Tom knows better than to respond.

"The room's metal detector indicates that you have two recording devises somewhere on your person. Please put them both on my desk."

Maureen removes one from under her loosely fitting blouse and another from within a hollowed-out notebook on her lap. Sitting down again, she crosses her previously uncrossed legs.

Tom continues. "With your acceptance, mine will be the official recording of this conversation.

Educate me as to your knowledge pertaining to the 1973 Native American uprising at Wounded Knee."

"What don't you already know? It started with intra-tribal bitching about who is getting what. A month or so before, a couple of town locals in Buffalo Gap killed Wesley Bad Heart Bull. When tribal access to the courthouse became restricted, fighting broke out between the riot police, AIM and protesters. The chamber of commerce building was literally destroyed.

Three weeks before the uprising, the reservation's tribal council had charged Dick Wilson with corruption and made the case for his impeachment.

Angered that Wilson had evaded impeachment with BIA's help, a coalition of local Oglala grouped around the "traditionals," the so-called "Oglala Sioux Civil Rights Organization (OSCRO)" asked AIM for help. AIM incited the Oglala and others to armed revolt against the United States of America. The traditionals went so far as to send a group to the United Nations asking to be recognized as a sovereign entity or be granted indigenous rights. Wounded Knee was a rebellion that had to be stopped before it inflamed others to demand rights.

On February 25th, at the request of the Bureau of Indian Affairs (BIA), 50 U.S Marshals were sent with orders to protect Dick Wilson and his Guardians of the Oglala Nation.

On February 27th, leaders from AIM including Russell Mead of the Oglala Sioux, Carter Camp, a member of the Ponca Tribe, and that pain in the ass, Dennis Banks, arrived to start trouble.

Within hours, we had roadblocks around Wounded Knee for 50 miles in every direction. In addition, Wilson stationed his GOONs beyond the federal boundaries."

Maureen stops to correct the record. "GOONs is the abbreviation for the Guardians of the Oglala Nation."

Tom Bass suppresses the urge to smile. Her passion for the topic is beginning to show and arrogance will not be far behind.

"We had them all boxed in with heavy reinforcements in motion. The uprising and AIM could have been eliminated then and there. Ultimately, we had fifteen armored personnel carriers armed with 50 caliber machine guns, helicopters, planes, and grenade launchers, 133,000 rounds of ammunition, federal marshals, FBI agents, and National Guard troops from five states within the reservation's boundaries. If given the word, AIM and its supporters would have all been dust. When AIM declared the territory around Wounded Knee to be the independent Oglala Nation, that was treason!"

Tom interrupts. "Why was that?"

"Because they're....." Maureen thinks better of what she is about to say. She does not complete the sentence.

Surprisingly, Tom chooses to answer for her. "They wanted BIA out of tribal affairs."

Maureen determinedly retakes the narrative.

"Once we got the Justice Department to remove Harrington Wood Jr., Kent Frizell had the electricity, water, and food supplies cut off and the new media barred from the reservation."

"Don't you think the exclusion of the media was a little heavy handed?"

"Come on Tom. You know damn well why. With figures like Brando and that bitch, Fonda, publically supporting these traitors, there was no other choice. Brando even went so far as to have some Apache actress accept his Oscar. Public sympathy made this siege drag out for 73 days. We could have ended it in a matter of hours and ...."

Again Tom finishes the sentence for her. "And again stained the character of our nation by re-enacting an ugly page of our history."

Quickly recovering from his tactile blunder, Tom asks.

"Who is Douglas Durham?"

The question is unexpected. Maureen had been assured that information concerning his identify had been classified as need to know only and covered by a national security designation. Apparently, the company had informants deep within the FBI.

"He is an FBI agent that had infiltrated AIM."

"How far in advance of Wounded Knee, had he been inserted?"

"That's a national security issue."

Then comes the question.

"Who ordered the assassination of a World Court Jurist?"

"Experts within more than one think tank had carefully researched the legality of doing it. They concluded that he had conspired to and liberated combatants through manipulation of the law. By so doing, he became a combatant himself in an ongoing armed rebellion against the United States. That negated his rights of citizenship. His actions speak for themselves. Almost every AIM member or Native American he defended has walked free."

"You still have not answered the question. Who ordered the assassination?"

"A patriot more powerful than you! The FBI wanted revenge for the murder of two of their agents. Operation Terminate has created a bond between our agencies. Who would have guessed that an Indian would have been so well known."

"That's not an answer" replies Tom.

Maureen fires back "That's the only answer you'll get."

"Fine!"

Tom's voice is that of controlled anger. "As far as the company is concerned, your Operation Terminate never existed. If what transpired ever surfaces, it will be denounced as a rogue operation and those involved will stand trial for murder. The assassination of such a prominent American – yes a prominent American – can never be laid at the company's door step. The President knew him personally. Be sure all the files are scrubbed. Nothing, and I mean nothing, that ever happened on the Pine Ridge Reservation ever involved the company!

I want an undated signed letter of resignation in your personnel file by tomorrow; unless you wish to do so now. And when the outside operatives you used surface, they are to be told that, if they ever reveal a word of this affair to anyone, they will be tried for murder and lose their pensions."

"You may not have to worry about pensions" responds Maureen.

"What?"

Getting up, Maureen answers. "They haven't reported in. Neither Wilson's men nor the BIA can find any trace of them."

The words escape Tom's lips. "Oh shit!"

Now smiling, Maureen gets up. "Do what you want, but there is no way in hell that you can call off Operation Terminate."

September 18, 1975, Black Hills

Somewhere within South Dakota's Black Hills, a figure, high on a ridge, signals. The horses move out from the shelter of the trees. The group is composed of four riders and eight horses. The extra horses signify that the journey will be long.

The ride quickly settles into hours of boredom. The darkness before the moon rises diminishes distractions. The hours drag by. Suddenly, a rider with horses appears out of the darkness. Horses are exchanged. Rider and spent horses disappear from where they came.

For Isaiah, boredom is gradually replaced by the begrudging knowledge that, while his legs may be primarily Sioux, his ass is not.

The trees are becoming fewer and the terrain is becoming progressively more difficult to negotiate. The wind finds its voice in the canyon-like terrain.

The cold is having its effect. Scarves wrapped around their necks and faces, the two riders in front are hunkering down in the saddle to minimize their exposure to the wind.

Isaiah's thoughts drifted through pages of his past. Eventually, he fixates on resentments born out of his sense of abandonment and the anger born out of it: anger that had found expression in sports. Football had been therapy. Others paid for the person not having been there.

Partial moonrise reveals the rolling hills to be gone. Steep gorges and cliffs dominate the landscape.

Paying homage to the cold, Isaiah reaches back and unties the straps of the knapsack. He pulls out a thick, full dress coat and puts it over the jacket. Holding the reins with his teeth, he thrust his right hand into its pocket for added warmth. The five-pointed medal in there told him whose coat he had sought refuge in.

Broken Lance breaks his train of thoughts.

"We have gone as far as we dare. Sunrise is an hour away. We need to find shelter."

Gilles R. G. Monif, M.D

September 17, 1975

Camp is a wind-created depression in the side of a steep gorge. The overhang provides both shade and concealment from above. The hard ground is a welcome relief from long hours in the saddle.

For Isaiah sleep is almost instantaneous. How long he slept he is not sure. Had not the demands of his stomach and bladder demanded immediate attention, the earth and he would have remained in mutual embrace longer.

First things first. Once the urgency of his bladder is placated, Isaiah's quest turns to food. Hanging from a tree branch wedged between the ground and the ceiling of the overhang are multiple cloth sacks containing fried bread, deer or buffalo jerky, and animal skin flasks containing water. Isaiah eats ravenously. The last time he had fried bread was just short of two decades. While there are four blanket rolls spread out on the ground, he is alone. Time passes. After a while, he again stretches out on the ground. He is about asleep when Broken Lance and the two other Native Americans reappear. Their hands contain three dead rabbits, an assortment of tubers and fire wood.

"We'll eat well once early evening comes". Seeing the puzzled look on Isaiah's face, Broken Lance continues, "After dusk, smoke is not easily detected."

The next hours are consumed by the creation of a shallow pit which then is lined with various sized stones. At dusk, a small fire is started. As the darkness intensifies the amount of wood increases until all that remains are the hot embers. The rabbits are gutted and stuffed with sage. Metal rods are passed through their bodies in such a way as to permit them to cook just above the heated stones and embers. The tubers are peeled, cut into slices, and eaten raw. Not all of the flasks contain water.

The cold returns quickly with the darkness. "When do we start again" is answered with "When the new horses get here. We could not keep them with us. They would have been seen."

The journey's continuation is demanding patience of which Isaiah finds himself in short supply. The distant cry of an owl is added to the night sounds. Broken Lance approaches Isaiah. "The horses are near."

The fire pit is covered with dirt. Where possible, signs of habitation are masked. The four horses are ready for mounting. The empty water bags are exchanged for filled ones.

After several hours, Broken Lance's horse approaches that of Isaiah.

"You need to dismount. From now on the trail becomes too narrow. We need to walk the horses. Stay close together. We still have a few hours of partial moonlight."

The riders and their mounts proceed in single file. For the first time, Isaiah looks closely at the white stallion whose theater he holds in his hand. The painted markings on his body single him out from the other horses. Black and blue thunder bolts run down his neck. On his forehead is a large circle with the colors of the four sacred directions. Inside the circle a black line runs from West to East and a red line runs from North to South. Where the lines meet is the image of a Cedar Tree.

The coat he is wearing had taught him that nothing that happens is by accident. On the final legs of the journey, he is being taken to his father's funeral on a special horse: his father's. That possibility, if not probability, comes almost simultaneously with a near encounter with the wrong end of the horse in front.

At the mouth of a small canyon, the group stops. Broken Lance imitates the calling of an Owl. The sound echoes off the rocks. Before the cry is repeated, it is answered. Broken Lance remounts his horse. He signals Isaiah to do the same. The other two riders turn their horses around and move in another direction.

Total silence is short lived. The sound of a horse slowly approaching penetrates the stillness. The only thing that moves is the water vapors of the exhaled breathe.

Out of the darkness, a single rider emerges. In size, his horse is the equal of Isaiah's mount. A large buffalo coat magnifies the volume of his silhouette.

Broken Lance makes two movements with his arms crossing his chest.

The figure stops and after a moment signals that they are to follow. Broken Lance and Isaiah follow in the rider some fifty feet ahead.

The three riders slowly make their way through the wind shaped canyon. Then the space between widens as the canyon merges with another that contains a dried creek bed. As they advance, Isaiah sees in the distance the outlines of what appear to be a number of buildings that face each other across what had once been a street.

Rusted machinery leans against a large cut in the side of the mountain. Decaying mining carts still stand on what might have been tracks. The sudden sound of wood collapsing startles Isaiah. The rider in front does not respond to the noise.

Broken Lance leans towards Isaiah and whispers. "This is an old gold mining town. It died in one day. The mountain refused to be violated any more and ate more than a hundred lives."

Pointing to a large pile of rocks, "That is the marker for those that tried to wretch from her the last veins of gold."

In front of what might have once been a hotel, the stranger dismounts. He approaches Isaiah who has dismounted in advance of Broken Lance.

The two men stand face to face. The stranger is equal to Isaiah in height and build. The large Buffalo coat tips the illusion of power in his favor.

"I am Wounded Buffalo. Out of honor for your father, I welcome you as Friend. Inside, we are waiting for you."

For Isaiah, the word, we, adds confusion.

Isaiah closely follows Wounded Buffalo. The wooden floor creaks as their combined weight tests them.

"Wait!"

The heel of the stranger's boot strikes the wooden floor twice. Out of the darkness below floor level, an irregular orange glowing light appears.

When lighted, the torches reveal that ten feet from where Isaiah is standing, the wooden floor abruptly ends. The greater part of the flooring has given way to a giant pit in the ground below. A domed structure covered with animal skins and a few blankets occupy the center of the pit.

"Come. The ladder is to your left. Have you ever been in a sweat lodge?"

"Yes", answers Isaiah. "When I was ten."

"If you are to present your father before the Great Mystery, you need to purge yourself of the evil accumulated in your other world. That nothing be hidden, you need to remove your clothes."

Isaiah begins undressing. Surprisingly the temperature is relatively mild. The reason quickly becomes apparent by men who enter the lodge carrying red hot stones on large forked sticks.

Isiah undresses. Only his under pant remain. The look from Wounded Buffalo tells him that it too most go.

Reluctantly, Isaiah complies. The last physical vestige of his other world comes to rest around his feet. He is given a loose fitting cloth robe to wear.

"Before you go in drink this water. When you are in the sweat lodge, you are to chew on red bark and the plant matter that is mixed with it."

Both men enter the lodge. A depression close to the entrance of the sweat lodge is filled with heated stones. Indicating the five large heated stones, Wounded Buffalo tells Isaiah "They are called stone people. Through them the voices of our Grandfathers speak to us. These stones symbolize the dwelling place of all."

Reaching over to his left, Wounded Buffalo takes what looks to be a large, hollowed out buffalo horn, dips it into a vessel containing water and sprinkles it on the "stone people". They hiss back.

For a minute, the two men just sit motionless as the warmth of the stones penetrates their bodies.

Then, Wounded Buffalo speaks, throwing more water on the heated stones. "Take a deep breath.

Hold it; now let it out slowly. Breathe in again.

Focus on your breathing."

Silence returns.

"For your Sioux ancestors, the interior of the sweat lodge is the womb of Mother Earth. Its darkness represents human ignorance. The hot stones are the coming of life. The stream is the creative force of the Universe being activated."

More water. More steam. A stone is removed and a new stone added. Perspiration becomes perfuse. Isaiah's robe now lies on the ground. The sweat from Isaiah's forehead falls on his eye lashes. His vision becomes blurry.

Wounded Buffalo's voice carries through the growing presence of steam. "Fire is for the rocks the undying light of the world.

Breathe in the earth's light. Let it cleanse you of your darkness. Let the evil winds within escape as you breathe out. Concentrate on your breathing."

The ensuing silence reinforces the stifling presence of heat.

Isaiah's thoughts recaptured the day of his law school graduation; one of the rare times that Georges was in attendance for more than a day. In the sweat lodge, words he long rejected found a more fertile reception. "Be careful of living too long in the wrong world. It corrupts. In turning our land, water, and air into depositories for the residues of our excessive consumption, we are destroying the kinship born of respect for all members within the Hoop of Nations."

The red bark that Isaiah has been chewing takes hold. If Wounded Buffalo speaks, Isaiah no longer hears him. Images from his life begin to take center stage. The pending case in front of the Appellate Court, the oil spill into the Delaware River, the clear cutting of virgin woods within a national park spin round and round. Reality blends. Triumphs of vanity begin taking on frightening forms. An owl, talons bared, descends, intent on plucking out his eyes. He moves only to be paralyzed by the sound of a large cedar tree as it descends to crush him. Then it speaks. "Be with the One".

His nakedness is now not just physical. The law, his law, that what he excelled at, have become a sterile game of words designed to disproportionally benefit its ringmaster at the expense of all others. Law of his father was never his law. Justice and greed cannot reside in the same room. It is, he is, a destroyer of creation!

Semi-conscious, Isaiah is abruptly taken from his vision by Wounded Buffalo's strong left hand. Lifting Isaiah to his feet, Wounded Buffalo says, "Your time to leave is now."

Their hair matted to their heads, both men stand facing one another within the sweat lodge. "The opening of the lodge faces east. If you have sweated out toxic events of your life, go through it and embrace the dawning of wisdom within you."

Isaiah emerges. Buckets of ice cold water poured over him shocking him back to this reality.

Broken Lance and another of the traveling group vigorously dry Isaiah. Sensing an emerging protest, Broken Lance says "We are just making sure the true color hasn't rubbed off. The true color of an Indian lies beneath that of his skin."

September 20, 1975

For the first time in days, his bed is not hard ground, but within the decaying building, the night brings its own trials and tribulations.

Sleep also escapes Broken Lance.

Seeing that Broken Lance is still awake, Isaiah asks "Why do you stay? Your two years at Dartmouth were your passport to a different life, certainly a less violent one."

Broken Lance's face emits a bitter-sweet smile. "I've thought about it many times. I could have taken the life path that you have traveled. If I had, I would have had to live in a world in which the Earth is viewed but as a resource. The writer, David Ipinia, described her as being an heirloom of which we are her guardians. Your people take possession of her, disfigure her, and then move on; leaving the mess they created for others to have to deal with. We can't do that. Being an Indian is walking on the earth so as to leave the smallest footprint. She is sacred to us. From the least stone to the greatest mountain, all is sacred. Her dirt is made of the dust and blood of our Grandfathers. When I walked the streets of Boston, everything felt cold. The measurement of that civilization is in building and technology, both of which are out of harmony with the earth and sky, but more importantly, their fellow man. Technology is fast becoming the opiate that prevents one from ever going on a spiritual vision quest.

I went East thinking that I would not be diverted from the teachings of the Grandfathers. I was so wrong. The temptation to taste the toxic beverage of greed and to become part of the living dead was too powerful. I knew I would die.

Standing Bear told us that the world is a library whose books are the stones, leaves, grass, brooks, birds, and animals. Taken me away from the land of my fathers, away from the oneness with all living things, the Indian in me would have died.

So, I chose to return to the reservation where the opportunity to do great deeds does not exist. What you see on reservations is mass suicide: self-poisoning done slowly with alcohol and drugs. Only in war, do we have the opportunity to escape the imposed societal barriers. War allows us to die with honor befitting the Grandfathers. In World War II, your father and mine fought against that which threatened the Oneness which is in all of us. My father died on Omaha Beach. Unlike your father, he never had his chance to honor his Grandfathers. The landing craft hit a mine. He was thrown into the water. Native Americas rarely know how to swim."

Broken Lance dips a cup with a broken handle into a rusty water bucket.

"I was born into a world in which the word, Indian, conjures up either the image of a drunk lying in a dark alley or a celluloid villain. No one hears the wisdom of the Grandfathers within. Our spirituality is gaged and discarded as irrelevant."

Broken Lance stops abruptly. "No, we are more than relevant! We are: the last guardian of the land, water, and sky and live with that knowledge unless consumed in the "soup".

The weapon of fear is used to justify our subjugation. What people do not understand, they fear. What they fear, they destroy. Your father was a great threat. He had a platform from which his demands for justice could have been ignored."

The first impulse of Isaiah's ego is to defend him against a growing sense of reduced self-worth. His second action is one of humility. Addressing Broken Lance, Isaiah speaks. "We are not so removed as you might think. "I too have paid a price for dark skin despite genes that embrace both colors. Being different does inspire fear and at times I have used it to my advantage. In the world of prep school football field, I was often the first dark skin player that they had encountered. I made certain that I left a memorable impression until I was reminded that it is hurt people who seek to hurt others. That has been part of the poison within me.

Sometimes it is not fear from without, but fear from within that becomes the destroyer. The golden rule of mediocrity is 'If you can't compete with the standard, destroy the standard'. When my anger was channeled into books, I became a gunner and would often get one of the two top marks in the class in every course.

I strove to be the standard. The words of my father had something to do with that; but, at the time, I was not willing to acknowledge it. To use imagery, I tried to become more cowboy than the cowboys.

I attained everything, but never felt accepted. Until now, I did not know how out of harmony I was with everything. The term societal toxicity fits. I guess what has separated father from me is that he had put his life in the service of others and in defense of what is truly civilization. I did the opposite."

Isaiah gets to his feet.

"Last night, more than sweat left me. It germinated within me seeds my father had planted.

In the papers White Cloud sent me was a brief to present to Congress. In it, he asked that the twenty Congressional Medals of Honors awarded to the soldiers of the Seventh U.S. Calvary after the Battle of Wounded Knee be rescinded. What I really liked is his use of Black Hawk and Chiksika words in describing the smoothness of our language that makes right look wrong and wrong look right. 'When a white man battles Indians and wins, it is called a victory. When they lose, it is called a massacre'. But it was always Wounded Knee that gave his pen purpose and power.

For him, there had been no true battle, just an excuse for genocide. He quoted someone that described bodies of countless women, women with babies, and children killed as far as two miles from the original camp. For him, the word battle when applied to Wounded Knee was a disgrace to our Nation's honor. Most soldiers were killed by friendly fire from the four Hotchkiss guns. He sought the dismantling of glorification of that which he felt must never happen again, genocide for reasons of race, color or religion."

Now in fuller possession of his words, Isaiah continues "A writer by the name of Thoreau once wrote 'The wilderness is the defense of civilization'. He understood what you have been saying."

Broken Lance nods in agreement. "Try and sleep. When night comes again, we'll be nearing journey's end."

September 21, 1975

Sleep comes at a great price. Isaiah tosses and turns. When sleep does come, dreams rob it of its serenity. His now world has put into question what, in the hours to come, he wil be asked to do.

In Broken Lance, Isaiah's brother of choice, he sees reflections of who he might be had not circumstances of the divorce dictated otherwise. The past is just that. The present is now. Isaiah looks around what was once a room. Determining which direction is East, he humbles himself. His knees firmly on the floor. He prays. The future is what it will be.

The day light hours creep slowly by. Finally, at dusk the horses arrive. Most of the marks are gone from Isaiah's white stallion. Only the white line remains.

Isaiah is anxious to begin, but Broken Lance waits until dusk settles into darkness.

Riding with the dark of the moon makes travel more difficult.

The landscape is again changing. Any trees once present have disappeared. The deep gullies and ravines again become mini-canyons. The riders again dismount and, in single file, lead their horses.

Coming to the confluence of three steep ravines, Broken Lance directs the cry of an owl down the center most alley. The response is silence. The sound is then directed down the one on the right. A distant animal cry responds. After a few hundred yards, the ravine constricts. The horses are backed up to where they can be turned around and led away.

Alone on foot, Broken Lance and Isaiah proceed until the ravine says no farther. Broken Lance gave two low pitched bird calls. He is about to repeat, when the end of a rope slips over the top of the obstruction.

Once on the other side, Broken Lance gathers up the rope. Picking up a beaded bag lying next to the other end of the rope, he extracts two pairs of gloves. He hands a pair to Isaiah. "Put them on. You'll need them. We're going to climb."

In the darkness, Isaiah is not sure, but it appears that the rope he is holding is made up of different colored smaller ropes.

Broken Lance hands Isaiah the rope. "From here we need to climb. Tie this around your waist and follow me."

The rock face in front of Isaiah rises at a nearly 60 degree angle. Progress is slow: at times very slow. The emptiness at his back makes thoughts of an alternative choice irrelevant. To get a better grip, his gloves are removed. Bad mistake. Somewhere well into the climb, Isaiah slips. The blood from the loss of skin makes grasping with his left hand more tenuous.

Gradually, the climb becomes easier. Suddenly Broken Lance gets on all fours and crawls forward, only to disappear into a black hole within the rock face.

The tunnel is not the work of nature. Instead of traveling up, it descends. Finally an orange glow in the darkness announces the near end of being four-legged.

Carved out of rock is a circular room with a high domed ceiling. The floor is uneven but smooth. Four elders in full ceremonial dress greet Isaiah and Broken Lance. Given their ages, Isaiah reasons that there is no way they could have made that climb. Wherever it is, there is another way to this Power Place to which he is not entitled.

Within the room, a circle marked by the placement of a number of stones mimics the room's perimeter. Four larger painted boulders mark the sacred directions. Within the Sacred Circle is a raised wooden scaffold containing his father's body.

An elder speaks directly to Broken Lance who turns and translates his words to Isaiah.

"They are telling you that the culture of the Lakota Sioux, your father's culture, is the fire of survival, but its flame grows ever weaker with time. The false rulers of the world want only to conquer the Earth, making her their slave. Having lost their harmony with nature, their kinship with living things, including two-legged creatures like us, weakens. They do not profit from what we learned over thousands of years from plants, non-human animals, and the stars: the formula for eternal survival. The web of life has many threads. Two legged creatures are but one thread that is bound together with the many. All things within the Great Mystery's creation are conceived in harmony and interdependency. Every time a species is irrevocably lost, part of creation is diminished. If the fire is extinguished before its flame is transferred to the souls of others, the Hoop of Nations will one day be no more."

Ceremoniously, one by one, the four elders enter the Circle and proceed to position themselves at the Four Directions within the circle and wait.

Broken Lance takes command. "The sacred circle that you are asked to travel to honor your father assumes the principles of unity and renewal of all of life's processes. You will enter through the East Portal and unite with your father. Then take his essence through the four directions. Examine him in the light of each direction's animal symbol."

What Broken Lance does not say, but that Isaiah knows from his days on the reservation, is that father's proximity to being united with Mother Earth makes him the Spirit of Below and his soul symbolizes the Spirit Above. Isaiah must become the Spirit Within.

Isaiah enters the Sacred Circle and moves directly to its center where his father lays. The poles supporting the scaffold are decorated by small painted drawings portraying his father's life deeds: a figure with a bow, a lance, books, and stars, among others. Georges' partially nude body has been washed and painted with a white dye, except where the two bullet wounds are. They are painted red. His long grey and black hair has been braided and two eagle feathers are tied in it. Isaiah reaches into a jacket pocket and adds the third eagle feather from White Cloud.

His father's red stone pipe is next to him. As instructed by White Cloud, kneeling next to the body of his father, Isaiah fills it with tobacco that he had brought with him and lights it. Taking a draw and exhaling the smoke, he raises the pipe as an offering to the East. Then, he pulls the yellow ribbon from those attached to the pipe. He carefully places it on his father's chest. The yellow ribbon points East. He repeats the symbolic tobacco offerings to the South, the West, and lastly the North, pulling each time the red, black, and white ribbons respectively. With the ribbons on the body pointing in the four sacred directions, he then closes his eyes. Turning his face upwards, he holds this position for a long time. Then, he brings his head down until it touches the wooden floor. It stays there for an even longer period of time.

Isaiah gets up awkwardly and walks to the edge of the scaffolding, not sure if he had done it right; but if he had, his father's physical body will no longer keep his soul from soaring.

The hand in his pocket reminds him that there is something, not pre-ordained, that he intended to do. He walks back and places the five-pointed medal with its bright blue ribbon at the center of the four direction ribbon. He bends down and says his goodbyes.

Getting up is difficult. His body is spiritually one of lead. Slipping back into memories of summers long forgotten and lessons lost, that he now understands. Isaiah speaks.

"I thank you, father. I am grateful. You gave me the reservation as your surrogate presence in my life. It is now my time to ground ordinary space into their cosmos of timelessness."

With steadfast deliberation, Isaiah moves towards the East portal. The elder there blocks his progress. His English is that of an educated man. "Death is passing from one world into another. The sacred circle you now travel to honor your father assumes the principles of unity and ongoing renewal of all of life's processes. Using the portal's animal, think of your father. When you have done so, I will accompany you to the South direction. At each of the sacred directions, another elder stationed there will step forward. You are to speak of your father through the portal's spirit. The Elder will then join us as we move to the next sacred direction."

And so it is done.

As the group comes again to the East, each elder says something in the Oglala tongue and exits, fading into the darkness of an adjoining space. Isaiah exits, only to be blocked by Broken Lance.

"If the Spirit Within moves you, place the 12th stone in line with the others and close the Sacred Circle of the Hoop of Nations."

The last stone in place, Isaiah retreats into the darkness of the adjacent spaces. The first seven steps are fine. Then, from deep within him, it surges. He fights it, but fails. Tears of shame and those of love stain his checks

September 22, 1975

Welcomed sleep comes quickly and ends too soon. "It is time to go."

Getting up, Isaiah puts his hand on Broken Lances arm. "Can I call you my Brother/Friend; no Brother and Friend?"

Broken Lance smiles. "Bounds of friendship, steeled by fire of actions, are stronger than those of blood. Let me tell you My Brother, that 'the light within your eyes is where the Universe dwells. When you are at the center within you, and I am in that place within me, we shall be one.' Those are the words Crazy Horse spoke to Sitting Bull three days before he was assassinated."

The two men tightly embrace.

Isaiah asks, "Was I ever given an Indian name?

Broken Lance shakes his head. "Only your father or Chief can give you one, but when you were on the reservation, some of the young boys called you, Horse That Kicks. But, here is a name that is now free; Snow Eagle. If you take it, you must live to fulfill the vision of the giver."

Isaiah walks back into the great room. His father's body is gone. Only the ashes of the scaffold remain. The void within is felt; yet, Isaiah is owned by an internal tranquility that has escaped him most of his life.

Broken Lance enters holding a fur lined hood that will cover his face. "Leaving will be easier than coming here."

Isaiah takes the hood from Broken Lance's hand. "No, let me put it over my eyes myself. I have lived so long blinded that temporary loss of physical sight is almost welcomed."

Putting the hood over his head, Isaiah adds "Within the hood, I see better than before."

Broken Lanced carefully leads the sightless Isaiah through interconnecting rooms.

"Stop here."

Isaiah hears the creaking of a winch as something is lifted up a great distance.

"It took 50 years to persuade this mountain to permit this. Step forward. The floor is a wobbly. Reach out with your right hand. Move your hand a little more to the right. You'll find a wood railing. Now seize it tightly. You are going down. Once you get to the bottom, someone will be there for you. I'll be right after you."

As the creaking noise becomes distant, Isaiah thinks that there can be but one reason for all these elaborate precautions. "I'm probably the first individual with any non-Native American blood to have passed through this scared space."

September 22, 1975

Broken Lance helps him into the saddle.

"My father's horse?" asks Isaiah.

"Your father's stallion" replies Broken Lance.

The two ride together for a number of hours. Finally, Isaiah speaks.

"White Cloud was my father's Brother/Friend. Thank you for being mine."

Broken Lance answers. "We are true Brothers."

"Thank you. In one week, I am changed..."

Broken Lance interrupts. "Only because you now see better the wisdom of the Grandfathers and the gifts they hope to impart to all."

The scent of cedar trees is there long before Isaiah's hood is removed. He is free. The anger and resentment he has harbored all these years is gone: gone like the vapor of one's breath on a cold winter night.

Isaiah shouts: "A life that had been lived in black and white is now in full color. I taste the morning. I hear as if for the first time. I feel complete. I have found my real world.

Thank you God. I am deeply aware of who I am. Not me, but me within your Hoop of Nations."

Isaiah leans back in the saddle. He drops the reins. Arms outstretched to the side, he gives voice to the words of Gandhi "God let me be the change I want to see in the world."

His exhilaration defies words. The energy is transmitted to his father's horse. His strides lengthen; then he breaks into a running gallop. Broken Lance's horse is hard pressed to keep up.

Then, they hear it.

Broken Lance shouts, "You go right and I'll go left. They can only chase one of us."

Both riders turn their horses and depart in different directions. Isaiah and his father's stallion race towards nearby woods. They crash through the underbrush and penetrate deep into the safety of the trees. Thirty-caliber bullets chew into the earth as they chase Broken Lance across the open meadow.

 # EPILOGUE

January 3, 1881

*In an editorial response to the Wounded Knee Massacre, Frank Baum wrote in the Aberdeen Saturday Pioneer:

"The Pioneer has before declared that our only safety depends upon the total extermination of Indians. Having wronged them for centuries, we had better, in order to protect our civilization, follow it up by one more wrong and wipe these untamed and untamable creatures from the face of the earth. In this lies the future safety for our settlers and soldiers who are under incompetent command. Otherwise, we may expect future years to be as full of trouble as those have been in the past."

Mr. Baum was later to write The *Wonderful Wizard of Oz.*

"In a dying world, when the last tree has been cut, all the rivers poisoned and the last fish caught only then will people realize that they cannot eat money."

Gilles R. G. Monif, M.D

A Cree Saying

If Crazy Horse, Sitting Bull, Spotted Elk, Red Cloud, and Standing Bear, among many others, could speak to us, they would warn us that, in our daily abuse of the earth and sky, we are moving away from that formula that guaranteed eternal survival. Each day, a new species is forever lost, contracting the Hoop of Nations ever smaller. Unless we listen to the words of the Grandfathers, a day will come when the time of two legged animals is no more."

*Citation listed is derived from the information gathered by Wikipedia.